Days With Frog and Toad

by Arnold Lobel

An I CAN READ Book

SCHOLASTIC INC.
New York Toronto London Auckland Sydney

For Liz Gordon

ISBN 0-590-40109-2

45 44 43 42 41 40 39 38   2 3 4 5 6 / 0

Printed in the U.S.A.

Contents

Tomorrow

Toad woke up.
"Drat!" he said.
"This house is a mess.
I have so much work to do."

Frog looked through the window.
"Toad, you are right,"
said Frog. "It is a mess."

Toad pulled the covers
over his head.

"I will do it tomorrow,"
said Toad.
"Today I will take life easy."

Frog came into the house.
"Toad," said Frog,
"your pants and jacket
are lying on the floor."

"Tomorrow," said Toad
from under the covers.

"Your kitchen sink
is filled with dirty dishes,"
said Frog.

"Tomorrow," said Toad.

"There is dust on your chairs."

"Tomorrow," said Toad.

"Your windows need scrubbing,"
said Frog.
"Your plants need watering."

"Tomorrow!" cried Toad.
"I will do it all tomorrow!"

Toad sat on the edge
of his bed.

"Blah," said Toad.
"I feel down in the dumps."

"Why?" asked Frog.

"I am thinking
about tomorrow,"
said Toad.
"I am thinking about
all of the many things
that I will have to do."

"Yes," said Frog,
"tomorrow will be
a very hard day for you."

"But Frog," said Toad,
"if I pick up my pants
and jacket right now,
then I will not have to
pick them up tomorrow, will I?"

"No," said Frog.
"You will not have to."

Toad picked up his clothes.
He put them in the closet.

"Frog," said Toad,
"if I wash my dishes right now,
then I will not have to
wash them tomorrow, will I?"

"No," said Frog.
"You will not have to."

Toad washed and dried his dishes.
He put them in the cupboard.

"Frog," said Toad,
"if I dust my chairs
and scrub my windows
and water my plants right now,
then I will not have to
do it tomorrow, will I?"

"No," said Frog. "You will not
have to do any of it."

Toad dusted
his chairs.

He scrubbed
his windows.

He watered
his plants.

"There,"
said Toad.
"Now I feel better.
I am not
in the dumps anymore."

"Why?" asked Frog.

"Because I have done
all that work," said Toad.
"Now I can save tomorrow
for something that I really want to do."

"What is that?" asked Frog.

"Tomorrow," said Toad,
"I can just take life easy."
Toad went back to bed.
He pulled the covers
over his head
and fell asleep.

The Kite

Frog and Toad went out
to fly a kite.
They went to
a large meadow
where the wind was strong.
"Our kite will fly up and up,"
said Frog.
"It will fly all the way up
to the top of the sky."

"Toad," said Frog,
"I will hold the ball of string.
You hold the kite and run."

Toad ran across the meadow.
He ran as fast as his short legs
could carry him.
The kite went up in the air.
It fell to the ground with a bump.
Toad heard laughter.
Three robins were sitting in a bush.

"That kite will not fly,"
said the robins.
"You may as well give up."

Toad ran back to Frog.
"Frog," said Toad,
"this kite will not fly.
I give up."

"We must make a second try,"
said Frog.
"Wave the kite over your head.
Perhaps that will make it fly."

Toad ran back across the meadow.
He waved the kite over his head.

The kite went up in the air
and then fell down with a thud.
"What a joke!" said the robins.
"That kite will never
get off the ground."

Toad ran back to Frog.
"This kite is a joke," he said.
"It will never get off the ground."

"We have to make
a third try," said Frog.
"Wave the kite over your head
and jump up and down.
Perhaps that will make it fly."

Toad ran across
the meadow again.
He waved the kite
over his head.
He jumped up and down.
The kite went up in the air
and crashed down into the grass.

"That kite is junk,"
said the robins.
"Throw it away and go home."

Toad ran back to Frog.
"This kite is junk," he said.
"I think we should
throw it away and go home."

"Toad," said Frog,
"we need one more try.
Wave the kite over your head.
Jump up and down
and shout UP KITE UP."

Toad ran across the meadow.
He waved the kite over his head.
He jumped up and down.
He shouted, "UP KITE UP!"

The kite flew into the air.
It climbed higher and higher.

"We did it!" cried Toad.

"Yes," said Frog.
"If a running try
did not work,
and a running and waving try
did not work,
and a running, waving,
and jumping try
did not work,
I knew that
a running, waving, jumping,
and shouting try
just had to work."

The robins flew out of the bush.
But they could not fly
as high as the kite.
Frog and Toad sat
and watched their kite.
It seemed to be flying
way up at the top of the sky.

Shivers

The night was cold and dark.
"Listen to the wind
howling in the trees," said Frog.
"What a fine time for a ghost story."

Toad moved deeper into his chair.

"Toad," asked Frog,
"don't you like to be scared?
Don't you like to feel the shivers?"

"I am not too sure," said Toad.

Frog made a fresh pot of tea.
He sat down
and began a story.

"When I was small," said Frog,
"my mother and father and I
went out for a picnic.
On the way home we lost our way.
My mother was worried.
'We must get home,' she said.
'We do not want to meet
the Old Dark Frog.'
'Who is that?' I asked.

'A terrible ghost,'
said my father.
'He comes out at night and eats
little frog children for supper.'"

Toad sipped his tea.
"Frog," he asked,
"are you making this up?"

"Maybe yes and maybe no,"
said Frog.

"My mother and father
went to search for a path,"
said Frog.
"They told me to wait
until they came back.
I sat under a tree and waited.
The woods became dark.
I was afraid.
Then I saw two huge eyes.
It was the Old Dark Frog.

He was standing near me."

"Frog," asked Toad,
"did this really happen?"

"Maybe it did
and maybe it didn't,"
said Frog.

Frog went on with the story.
"The Dark Frog pulled
a jump rope out of his pocket.

'I am not hungry now,'
said the Dark Frog.
'I have eaten too many
tasty frog children.
But after I jump rope
one hundred times,
I will be hungry again.
Then I will eat YOU!'"

"The Dark Frog tied one end
of the rope to a tree.
'Turn for me!' he shouted.
I turned the rope for the Dark Frog.
He jumped twenty times.
'I am beginning to get hungry,'
said the Dark Frog.

He jumped fifty times.
'I am getting hungrier,'
said the Dark Frog.
He jumped ninety times.
'I am very hungry now!'
said the Dark Frog."

"What happened then?"
asked Toad.

"I had to save my life,"
said Frog.
"I ran around
and around the tree
with the rope.
I tied up
the Old Dark Frog.
He roared and screamed.

I ran away fast."

"I found my mother and father,"
said Frog.
"We came safely home."

"Frog," asked Toad,
"was that a true story?"

"Maybe it was
and maybe it wasn't,"
said Frog.

Frog and Toad sat
close by the fire.
They were scared.
The teacups shook
in their hands.
They were having the shivers.
It was a good, warm feeling.

The Hat

On Toad's birthday
Frog gave him a hat.
Toad was delighted.

"Happy birthday," said Frog.

Toad put on the hat.
It fell down over his eyes.

"I am sorry," said Frog.
"That hat is much too big for you.
I will give you something else."

"No," said Toad. "This hat
is your present to me. I like it.
I will wear it the way it is."

Frog and Toad went for a walk.
Toad tripped over a rock.
He bumped into a tree.
He fell in a hole.
"Frog," said Toad,
"I can't see anything.
I will not be able to wear
your beautiful present.
This is a sad birthday for me."

Frog and Toad
were sad
for a while.
Then Frog said,
"Toad, here is what you must do.
Tonight when you go to bed
you must think
some very big thoughts.
Those big thoughts will make
your head grow larger.
In the morning
your new hat may fit."

"What a good idea," said Toad.

That night when Toad went to bed
he thought the biggest thoughts
that he could think.
Toad thought about
giant sunflowers.
He thought about tall oak trees.
He thought about high mountains
covered with snow.

Then Toad fell asleep.
Frog came into Toad's house.
He came in quietly.

Frog found the hat
and took it to his house.

Frog poured some water on the hat.
He put the hat
in a warm place to dry.
It began to shrink.
That hat grew smaller and smaller.

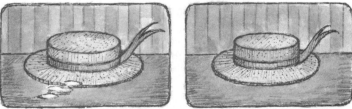

Frog went back to Toad's house.
Toad was still fast asleep.
Frog put the hat back on the hook
where he found it.
When Toad woke up in the morning,
he put the hat on his head.

It was just the right size.

Toad ran to Frog's house.
"Frog, Frog!" he cried.
"All those big thoughts
have made my head
much larger.
Now I can wear your present!"

Frog and Toad went for a walk.
Toad did not trip
over a rock.
He did not bump into a tree.
He did not fall
in a hole.

It turned out to be
a very pleasant
day after Toad's birthday.

Alone

Toad went to Frog's house.
He found a note on the door.
The note said,
"Dear Toad, I am not at home.
I went out.
I want to be alone."

"Alone?" said Toad.
"Frog has me for a friend.
Why does he want to be alone?"

Toad looked through the windows.
He looked in the garden.
He did not see Frog.

Toad went to the woods.
Frog was not there.
He went to the meadow.
Frog was not there.
Toad went down to the river.
There was Frog.
He was sitting on an island
by himself.

"Poor Frog," said Toad.
"He must be very sad.
I will cheer him up."
Toad ran home.
He made sandwiches.
He made a pitcher of iced tea.

He put everything
in a basket.

Toad hurried
back to the river.
"Frog," he shouted,
"it's me.
It's your best friend, Toad!"
Frog was too far away to hear.
Toad took off his jacket
and waved it like a flag.
Frog was too far away to see.
Toad shouted and waved,
but it was no use.

Frog sat on the island.

He did not see or hear Toad.

A turtle swam by.
Toad climbed on the turtle's back.
"Turtle," said Toad,
"carry me to the island.
Frog is there.
He wants to be alone."

"If Frog wants to be alone,"
said the turtle,
"why don't you leave him alone?"

"Maybe you are right," said Toad.
"Maybe Frog does not
want to see me.
Maybe he does not want me
to be his friend anymore."

"Yes, maybe," said the turtle
as he swam to the island.

"Frog!" cried Toad.
"I am sorry for all
the dumb things I do.
I am sorry for all
the silly things I say.
Please be my friend again!"
Toad slipped off the turtle.
With a splash, he fell in the river.

Frog pulled Toad
up onto the island.
Toad looked in the basket.
The sandwiches were wet.
The pitcher of iced tea was empty.
"Our lunch is spoiled," said Toad.
"I made it for you, Frog,
so that you would be happy."

"But Toad," said Frog.
"I *am* happy. I am very happy.
This morning
when I woke up
I felt good because
the sun was shining.
I felt good because
I was a frog.
And I felt good because
I have you for a friend.
I wanted to be alone.
I wanted to think about
how fine everything is."

"Oh," said Toad.
"I guess that is a very good reason
for wanting to be alone."

"Now," said Frog,
"I will be glad *not* to be alone.
Let's eat lunch."

Frog and Toad
stayed on the island
all afternoon.
They ate wet sandwiches
without iced tea.
They were two close friends
sitting alone together.